Please Don't Let Me Be Misunderstood

N. NICHELLE

Please Don't Let Me Be Misunderstood. Copyright 2021 by N. Nichelle. All rights reserved. No part of this publication may be reproduced, distributed, or transmitted in any form or by any means, including photocopying, recording, or other electronic or mechanical methods, without the prior written permission of the publisher, except in the case of brief quotations embodied in critical reviews and certain other noncommercial uses permitted by copyright law.

For permission requests, write to the publisher, addressed "Attention: Permissions Coordinator," 205 N. Michigan Avenue, Suite #810, Chicago, IL 60601. 13th & Joan books may be purchased for educational, business or sales promotional use. For information, please email the Sales Department at sales@13thandjoan.com.

Printed in the U. S. A.

First Printing, November 2021.

Library of Congress Cataloging-in-Publication Data has been applied for.

ISBN: 978-1-953156-46-4

TABLE OF CONTENTS

"Don't go down in the belly of the beast"

—*THE PREACHER*

"It ain't what you doing, its what it looks like that's what they gonna talk about"
—*GRANDMA*

"They killing ya'll!"

—*WADE*

"Guess white folks don't have no warrants"

—*WOO*

"I don't need no man loving me to death"

—*MACK*

"We as a people used to look out for our own and feel safe around each other not tear each other down"

—*KHALIL*

PROLOGUE

W OO IS AN example of how sometimes we can be our own antagonist. She shows how the mind can be our worst enemy, the enemy we cannot outrun and ton defeat we must go within. Overcoming self is when we find our true power.

"I write for young girls of color, girls
who don't even exist yet, so that there
is something there for them when
they arrive"

— Ntozake Shange

CHAPTER 1

T HE ELEVATOR DOORS made a moaning sound as they creaked open. A short, bald preacher was blocking the now open doors, a worn Bible in his hand with notes and placement keepers hanging from it. A badge hung from his neck: *Visitor Richmond Jail.* He used his worn handkerchief to pat at the sweat now glistening on his forehead as he looked her up and down.

The girl was new, he could tell. He'd been preaching at this jail one night a week for the past three years, and this was his first time seeing her. She was too delicate to be here; this was no place for the timid, which her soft eyes showed her to be. In this case, it didn't help that she was so beautiful. She had soft brown skin the color of a new copper penny, and she was short, probably only five feet tall even. She was not much at the top but made up for it as she rounded out at the hips, thighs, and butt so that she stretched the bright red fabric of her scrubs. She had a fresh innocent face with soft features and plump lips. A sunken old scar about three inches long stood out of place under the out-side corner of her left eye. She had waist-length locs pulled back into a ponytail that filled the stuffy elevator with an intoxicating scent, and soft baby hairs framed her face and clung to the nape of her neck.

The older, light brown nurse beside her wore no expression, mastered by over ten years of working corrections. She'd seen a lot and been through a lot, so not much surprised her, and almost nothing garnered a reaction from her.

The preacher, lost in his worried thoughts, hadn't noticed the doors open, and now they were closing back up.

The older sister impatiently reached around him to press *one* again, knowing it was likely to take the doors a while to open up once more.

The preacher spoke up.

"Please wait, young sister! Don't go down in the belly of the beast!"

Willow stood quiet but interested. *I'm here now.*

The doors were open again, and Turner, the nurse who was training her, was getting off with or without her. She sidestepped the man and gave him a helpless shrug.

"Well, God bless you, little sister," he called out before the doors re-shut. *You'll need it.*

The older nurse went by Turner.

"Last names only," she had told Willow.

She would have to adjust to going by Woo. Her last name itself told the story behind her sleepy eyes and saved her the explanation – her father was part Korean.

Turner pounded a button attached to a speaker on the wall.

"Don't nothin' work 'round here," she mumbled as she pressed harder.

"Control?" a voice came through the speaker.

"Open 105." Turner spoke into the box.

Woo watched closely. Turner was far from bad looking—just very bland. Her brown skin was blemish free yet dull, and she rarely smiled—or frowned, for that matter. The only interesting thing Woo could find on her was her extremely wide hips.

There was a loud buzz, and Turner slung the heavy door open, thrust it back, and held it open as she pulled her detox med cart through.

The second Woo stepped over the threshold of lock-up, it was as if someone had snatched the air out of the place.

Cells lined both sides of the sordid hall, and a mixture of body odor, shit, and some type of air freshener hung heavily like a cloak.

"Female on the floor," Turner said robotically. She peered over her rectangular glasses at Woo. "That lets them know to get decent, but they never do."

No sooner had she said that than Woo looked up to see the inmate directly ahead of them turn and take a piss as if they were invisible. She wiped her now sweaty forehead as Turner fanned herself with her clipboard.

"No airflow," she sighed. She had assumed the young girl's visible sweat and overall look of discomfort was due to the lack of fresh air on the hot floor. Truth was, that was only the half of it; Woo was drained emotionally. She was an extreme empath, and the raw, passionate emotions surrounding her were sucking all of the energy from her, and it was only intensified due to the lack of fresh air. Such was the reason she could be considered a hermit. Even the simplest outing would exhaust her. However, this was extreme. She had periods where she felt fine—almost normal, even sociable—followed by weeks of solitude to recharge.

She gripped the wall, grimacing at the way her hand stuck to the grime as she steadied herself. She forcefully blocked out the noises in her head and willed her energy back.

Woo's eyes adjusted to the dimly lit hall and noticed all the brown arms hanging through the bars. As far as she could see, only about three sets of arms were white.

A tall, buff, walnut brown deputy appeared, looking at his watch as if he had someplace better to be. His gold badge read *Carter*.

"Who y'all need?" he asked in an uninterested tone.

Turner read off her paper.

"Cells 6, 12, 18, 22, and 24 for evening detox." She didn't bother to introduce the two. They could do that on their own time, that was if the girl stayed long enough. Besides, Carter had enough on his plate, and everybody knew he didn't take anything seriously, she figured.

Turner checked vitals and gave out medications while Woo took note.

"That's a lot of red, huh?" a deep voice asked.

Woo looked up so high her neck craned until she saw the eyes of a huge, medium brown man who was covered in tattoos from his face on down.

"If I was you, I wouldn't wear that color no more." He threw his med cup through the bars, just missing her feet, as opposed to dropping it in the trash bin on the cart like everyone else had, all disrespect intended.

She turned her head for the deputy, but he had disappeared, leaving them to fend for themselves.

The alcoholics had the shakes and delirium, and the heroin addicts had body aches with diarrhea. The meth addicts had open sores covering their faces and arms, and their ages didn't match their faces—the drugs added years they had yet to experience.

"Do we clean them?" she innocently asked as she peered in a cell where one addict had shit everywhere but in the toilet. The smell made her hold her breath. Her last job was at a nursing home, if someone messed themselves or made any other type of mess, the nurses and aides cleaned them. There were no aides here, so she figured they would go in and change the man and clean his cell.

Turner scrunched her face up, repulsed at the thought.

"Girl, no. Once the deputy gets tired of smelling it, he'll get tossed in the shower some kinda way."

The addicts begged for stronger medications, and Woo peered up over Turner's shoulder as she dropped two Tylenols and a Meclizine pill for nausea in the pill cup emotionlessly.

One young man that pulled at her heartstrings was an eighteen-year-old who looked as if he should've been in high school. Turner had walked on, not noticing or caring Woo wasn't following her anymore.

"I can't wait to get out tomorrow; my homie got a pack waiting on me," he said as he scratched his arms.

"Why, after you just went through detox? You're so young, and you got your whole life ahead," she told him.

"Once an addict, always an addict." He shrugged.

"I disagree. That's what they tell you. Mind over matter. Everything is created twice. First in the mind, next in the physical, and what you tell yourself is what you become. If you wake up every morning saying you're just an addict, that's all you'll ever be... If only you knew how strong your words are."

She got off her soapbox at what sounded like clapping behind her. She turned to see the man lying in the bottom bunk with his eyes transfixed on her, his hands rising and falling under the thin sheet.

"Oh, hell no! Stop! Is it worth being on the sex offender list? Cas I'ma tell on your nasty ass!" she bluffed, the shock causing her to forget she was to remain professional.

"Girl, I don't give a fuck. That's why I'm here!" He gave her a toothless grin.

She shuddered, turning back to the young boy.

"Think about what I said. It's never too late," she called as she backed away, not giving the old man anything else to look at, then rushed off to catch Turner, who was pulling her cart through the door despite the young girl not being with her. Turner didn't believe in babying her trainees; they wouldn't learn that way, she reasoned.

Turner took Woo through to Processing to show her how to do intakes.

"Most of them come off the streets and not on no medication since the last time they was here or off their psychiatric meds. Which could be days, months, or years. We try to get them back on soon as possible. Keyword *try*," Turner told her. "But first, come on; we got a sally port."

Woo followed Turner to the other side of Booking. She didn't know what a "sally port" was, but she was about to find out.

A young Black guy stood handcuffed while two White police officers laughed with the booking deputy.

"We basically make sure they're medically stable for jail. If it's something life threatening or critical, send them back out. Keep in mind the officers will lie to you so always do your own assessment," Turner told her. "Take the cuffs off him, please," Turner said to the officers with her hands on her hips.

Woo raised her eyebrow at the swelling and redness on the man's wrists as the cuffs were removed. *Damn, that's so unnecessary.*

After clearing him, Turner was about to walk off.

"What's that?" Woo peered at the man's face as a trickle of blood slid down from his matted 'fro.

Turner reached up and parted the man's hair with her hands and stepped back. With his hair now out of the way, the gash on his scalp was visible. He would need stitches at the least.

"Why didn't you say anything?" the booking deputy frantically yelled.

"The cops told me not to," the man said helplessly as both officers rolled their eyes.

Turner's poker face remained.

"Have him cleared at the ER first," she said, scribbling "REFUSED *due to scalp laceration. Needs to be medically cleared!*" on her sally port form and handing it to the officer, who rudely didn't take the form and let it drift to the floor.

"They just gone go dump him somewhere," Turner told her on their way to Medical.

"Huh." Woo scrunched her face, confused.

"When they have a simple charge and we refuse them, they supposed to take them to ER, but that don't always happen. Sometimes they'll take them and dump them out on the corner; we'll know if he don't come back."

Back in the outdated medical office, Woo sat beside Turner firing off questions even though she was supposed to be paying attention and learning how to use their computer system.

"I heard you tell that guy in lock-up we don't detox for crack. Why is that?" Woo asked.

"Since when White folks care about a crackhead? Majority of crack addicts in here are who? Exactly. Now all a sudden it's an opiate crisis, and yet we still the ones filling up places like this." Turner sighed.

"So what we do for them then?" Woo pressed.

"Nothin'," Turner said without looking up, done answering questions.

"What do we do about what?" a raspy voice coughed. It was Keene, the DOA over the Medical Department. He was barely there, and when he was, he ran out every twenty minutes for a smoke break. Hence the chronic, long-suffering cough that he ignored, sanitary precautions included. He smelled of smoke, Big Red gum, and heavy cologne. He only cared that they showed up to work and they had no medical-related deaths at the end of the month.

Woo later learned that hospital deaths didn't count—so if the person made it to the hospital and passed away due to something that happened at the jail, it didn't fall on them.

Turner ran things for him anyhow. In return, she did as she pleased. She made the schedule, plugging everyone in around what worked best for her. As he waited for an answer, he hovered so close over Woo's chair that she could feel his stomach pressing into her back. She looked up at him and back down to his stomach as she scooted her chair away with much attitude. He was always finding reasons to brush past too close or telling inappropriate jokes that bordered on the lines of sexist and racist.

"Well, a lot of them just don't care, so they get out and do the same shit that got them in here. We have resources, and they don't choose to use them." He had heard their conversation, just as she'd thought.

"Well, there are many inequalities such as education and housing, discrimination and…"

He put his hand up to stop Woo.

"Doesn't mean they can go out and commit crimes, correct?"

"A crime of survival, you say? In areas with a threatening police presence who, by the way, are not from said community?" Woo didn't feel like saying more, so she stopped. He, like many others of his kind, already knew this, but she couldn't make him care. She could see his face turning red as he frowned at her, upset that she wouldn't accept him talking down on her people.

It didn't take long for Woo to realize Turner and Keene had something going on. She was starting to get uncomfortable when alone with the two of them.

As if on cue, Turner stood, and they both walked in his office, closing the door behind them. Turner didn't come back out either, so Woo sat and stared at the clock until the exact second it was quitting time. She grabbed her large, clear tote and clocked out.

CHAPTER 2

"**G**IRL, WHAT, EVERYBODY in here fuckin'!" Houston laughed after Woo shared her suspicions of Turner and Keene. "Not me though. I mean, I do me. Just not in here cas all these niggas do is talk and I learned that the hard way."

Houston was truly a breath of fresh air. *Real* was the best way to describe her. She was a big girl and wore it well. She had light brown skin and a long, frizzy red weave, a beautiful soft face with a genuine smile, and long, rainbow stiletto nails. Medical was supposed to comply with the same dress code as the security staff, minus the uniform, but none of them did, and Keene let it slide as well. Houston was openly bi, a party girl, and she and Woo took to each other instantly. They both loved to laugh and did so all the while they were together, often making jokes of the most serious situations even when they shouldn't.

"Cabin fever," Woo concluded. "All these doubles and twelve-hour shifts – all we see is each other."

She finished her slice of pizza from the large she and Houston had gone half on. They shared a table in the break room, which contained six square tables, four vending machines, four couches, and a small, dirty kitchen. The only updated thing was the large plasma hanging on the wall.

"Speaking of Turner, her basic ass better give me the weekend off," Houston said as she bit into her pizza, silently making plans.

Woo nodded halfheartedly, caught up in a daze by Houston's colorful nails. She was now used to working in the jail and often used humor to get through her shifts.

Just then Idris, one of the deputies, walked into the break room. He had the smoothest light brown skin and intense eyes that seemed to look through Woo when she was in his presence. He had a silver streak that started at his hairline and went through his eyebrow, ending on the lashes on his left eye. Nobody seemed to know much about him—he'd transferred highly recommended from a maximum security prison the year before. His walk was a slow and confident stride, and he whistled as he approached their table.

"Wassup, Woo; wassup, Houston," he said in a low, deep voice.

"Heyyy," Houston sang as she threw her hand up with a flash of bright light from her nails.

"Hey, Idris." Woo smiled, glad to be set free from the trance Houston's nails had her in. She made a mental note to finally add some color to the basic coffin shape, amber nails that she always got.

Houston had already told her of the deputies and nurses sleeping with inmates and each other, male and female alike. She wasn't looking for anything at work or otherwise, so that didn't matter to her.

"You working overnight?" he asked, raising an eyebrow at her as he sat on one of the break room couches.

"Yup, what floor you on?" she asked him.

"Five." He slowly smiled.

"I'll be up on my rounds." Woo glanced to see if Houston was paying any attention, but she was busy securing her plans for when she got off at eleven.

On slow nights, Woo usually hung out and ate snacks with Idris either in Medical or on his floor. Despite his no nonsense demeanor, he was a lot of fun.

All the medical staff had dispersed down to Woo and Mack, an older Black woman with mahogany brown skin. She worked a couple nights a week when Houston was off. Working with Mack was cool, minus all the complaining she did.

Mack was wiping down her area, and her area only, with sanitizing wipes. The whole time she wiped, she fussed about how "Somebody else should do it for once."

It didn't bother Woo. She was meticulously neat, so she knew it wasn't her Mack was referring to.

Once Mack was satisfied with her work, she set out her snacks and made herself comfortable. She called one of her friends and logged in on her Facebook account, where she would be until shift change in the morning.

Woo didn't mind. She regarded Mack like an auntie and preferred to keep moving through the night anyway to keep from getting sleepy. She did the floor tasks, and Mack would hold down the clinic. Well, until 3:00 a.m., which Mack referred to as the "ungodly hour," so it was only right she slept through it.

Woo grabbed one of the bulky radios and clipped it to her hip.

"I'll be back!" she hollered as she headed for the door.

"Mm-hmm, child." Mack slid Woo's abandoned chair over and propped her feet on it. "Hit the light on your way and take your time, honey."

Since Woo made a habit of getting all her work done in the first half of her double shift, her schedule was clear for now, granted the unexpected didn't occur. She had a habit of racing the clock and was compulsive when it came to time, always rushing for no reason. *Be in the present* is what her grandma used to say to her.

Idris was always placed on the rowdy floors, yet he maintained calm order. It was dark and somewhat quiet up on the fifth floor except for the humming of the dusty old fans on opposite sides of the floor, blowing stale air.

She smiled at the sight. Most deputies hoarded all the fans they could find in their offices, even stealing them from the other floors and leaving the inmates to fend for themselves.

Idris's theory was they were calmer when it was cool and dark. He even played soft music once the TVs went off.

She quietly made her way to the deputy's office, careful not to make a sound even though the inmates could always tell when she was on the floor. They didn't have to see her; they knew the nurses by smell, sound of footsteps, and God knows how else, but they always knew.

She leaned against the doorway as Idris slowly looked up at her. He took his time in everything he did. The lights in the office were off. The only light was the glare from the computer screen as a TV show streamed.

Woo flicked the lights on before stepping inside. She could hear her grandmother's voice: *"It ain't what you doing—it's what it look like that they gone talk about."* She didn't need anyone walking by and getting the wrong idea, adding her name to the rumor list.

"You started without me!" she squealed, faking hurt. *Motivation* was the show they watched together when they worked Monday nights.

"Calm down. I started it when I heard you coming through the gate." He playfully nudged her once she pulled up a chair beside him. He always smelled like a faint hint of Gaultier cologne and kept a fresh edge up. He pulled some snacks and two Sprites out of his bag and sat them on the desk.

"All is forgiven," she laughed. He often took notes of the snacks he saw her constantly sneaking and started bringing them for her.

The show ended, and the two sat making jokes and talking. Despite her holistic lifestyle, she had a terrible sweet tooth that her grandma had always blamed her mother for. On the rare occasions that her mother showed up, she showered Woo with candy and treats and left the usually reserved, quiet child hyped up on sugar. Her grandma didn't know when Woo asked for her mom if it was really the candy she wanted. Once she was old enough, she would walk to the corner store every chance she got to buy candy, and she kept a stash in her room, never wanting to go without again like the long periods of time when her mom went ghost.

Now even as a grown woman she snuck to eat her candy out of habit. She kept her work pockets stuffed with it and never was without anymore. She tried to balance it out so that her meals were pretty healthy, and she drank water like a fish; she accepted the fact that she just loved candy.

Woo slid her heavy nurse clogs off and wiggled her toes free inside her socks in front of the fan.

"Oh, hell no! Get your funky-ass feet from out the fan!" he laughed.

"My feet don't stink... they are sweaty though," she admitted. They were interrupted by the radio.

"Intake to Medical, we have a sally port," a gruff voice came through.

"10-4." Woo made a face at Idris. She stood and stretched, and he prepared to get up with her.

"I gotta do rounds then I can walk you down." He was very protective of her, and she appreciated the gesture.

"Nope, I'm good. Duty calls," she said as she rushed out.

Down in booking was another story this time of night/ early morning. It smelled of alcohol, vomit, and the strong mixture of cleaning solution the trustee had made and was mopping the floor with.

Irritation rode through her when she recognized who her sally port was. It was Carmack, a young Black man in a wheelchair. He had been born with cerebral palsy and was also severely autistic. He was a regular, always brought in on suspicion of being under the influence.

Even if that was so, back in the day if you were found drunk, they took you home. Now straight to jail, Mack had told her.

Carmack was homeless, his family whereabouts unknown since he didn't speak clearly. He spoke mostly gibberish and laughed randomly to himself. The crazy thing about him was that he couldn't walk, but he could climb and scale a wall like Spiderman.

Woo thought back to a few weeks before when she had gone to give him medicine but couldn't find him in his cell. She figured she had the wrong cell number and had Houston double check. Houston had come to her side to tell her in person, "Nope, girl, he *should* be right here in 16."

She had looked in and slowly peered up.

"What the fuck?" Woo looked up in disbelief. Carmack was practically on the ceiling, sneering at them with his arms and legs extended, nude.

"Is he pussy poppin' on the handstand?" Houston had asked in awe.

Woo had pressed her face into Houston's shoulder in laughter.

"This explains how his ass kept getting in the top bunk; I thought I was trippin'." Woo fanned herself.

Carmack usually refused his meds anyway, so she had left him a cup of cold water on the bars for when he came down.

That was weeks ago, and now he was back. She assessed him as she stole a glance at his breathalyzer report, which was normal.

"He's not drunk or nothin', just mentally impaired, but we knew that already." She tilted her head at the two White officers with their matching buzz cuts as she waited for a response.

"Right! So what ya'll charging him with?" demanded Sgt. Williams. She was a cocoa brown-skinned woman in her mid-forties whom Woo liked. She was quick to call out the officers for their bullshit.

The cops literally dragged people in who were in need of medical care, downplaying injuries or coercing them to withhold medical information. Just a few nights before, they'd dropped off a guy, completely leaving out the fact that he'd been tased multiple times. Before they could pull away, his eyes rolled into the back of his head, and he was on the floor. He'd been revived and sent to the E.R. after they reluctantly returned for him. Resisting arrest was his charge after arguing with the officers.

It terrified Woo deeply that those that enforced the laws had yet to learn them, being that "a citizen had the right to resist an unlawful arrest to the point of taking an officer's life if necessary." – Plummer v. State.

However, she understood whether they knew or not, not much would change for her people.

The two officers shared a conspiring look.

"Trespassing," the shorter one answered.

"You can't be serious. He's homeless!" Williams shouted.

The taller cop lowered his eyes to Carmack's ashy thighs and dingy boxers. His pants sat on his knees four sizes too big.

"Indecent exposure," he blurted out with a satisfied smile.

Woo rolled her eyes. "Oh, my God." She was ready for them to leave at this point. *At least now he can get a shower and something to eat.*

He had lost weight since he'd gotten out a few weeks ago. He'd stayed two months on a trespassing charge with a two hundred dollar bond he couldn't afford nor possibly understand. He smelled horrible, and his thick long locks were matting into four sections. He needed help, but he didn't belong in jail.

She whirled his wheelchair around so fast his head jerked up.

"Sorry." She patted his shoulder as he threw his head back, squealing excitedly in a childlike manner.

After Carmack was settled, Woo stayed in booking, watching TV with Williams in case any more intakes came in.

A loud slam followed by yelling came from over in lock-up.

"Come on, sound like they gone need a nurse," Williams said as she stood.

Out of habit, Woo peeked through the rectangle-shaped window on the door while they waited to be buzzed through. She saw the inmates in cells with shirts covering their faces. *Trifling asses. Somebody must've farted.*

The door opened, and she immediately wished it hadn't. Her eyes began to burn. She opened her mouth in shock, and instantly her throat felt as it was on fire.

Down the hall, Deputy Clark—who wasn't much taller than her at 5'6"—was attempting to pepper spray Cleveland, the inmate who'd warned her about wearing red on her first day.

Cleveland towered over Clark at 6'5", his hand wrapped around Clark's neck, lifting him in the air, his other hand holding back two other deputies who had shown up to help.

Williams, a veteran in these situations, shook her head, ashamed of her deputies, and pressed forward to gain control of the situation.

The seconds felt like minutes to Woo. She was panicking due to not being able to see where to go.

"Keep going. You almost there, watch your step." The inmates were verbally guiding her to the exit. She was humbly moved. *I'm giving them all Gatorade tomorrow.*

Once her hand found the button, and the door buzzed, she stumbled out of it. Strong hands caught her before she tripped, and Idris led her back up to the fifth floor.

"It burns," she openly cried. The tears that streamed down her face stung her cheeks.

"Calm down. You keep reactivating it." Idris dabbed her face with a tissue. He took advantage of the fact that she was blinded for the moment and studied her up close. He was quiet, composed, and obsessed over details. She had an innocence about her, no makeup anywhere on the pile of tissues she littered blindly all over the floor, each time missing the trash bin. She was vulnerable right now, dependent on him and, little did she know, he loved the control.

After her shift, she was drained mentally and physically. The force it took not to pick up so many strong emotions that night was difficult. When she got home, she had to release it usually in a hot shower with 432hz playing.

She ran her hand across her altar made to pay respects to her loved ones gone before her. It was beautifully decorated with an 8x10 photo of her grandma in the center in a vintage wooden frame and candles and fresh flowers on each side. She had a bowl of sage, incense, a bowl for offerings, and healing crystals on the altar as well. She yearned for her grandmother's guidance and wisdom right now. Was this the job for her?

Woo had found her grandmother passed away in her small armchair, slumped over, about eight months before. She'd since pushed the chair into her grandma's room and shut the door, though some mornings she woke to the door being ajar and her grandma's scent of bergamot and patchouli oil in the air.

All the women on her mother's side were different based on society's standards. Her grandmother was the natural healer, an empath as well, but she was a plant empath. She could grow anything and knew what the uses were – a self-taught botanist.

Woo was aware that she didn't possess that gift and had struggled to keep up all of her grandma's treasured plants after her passing. A few passed right behind her; it was pitiful. The energy in the brownstone hadn't been the same, and it was like they knew she was gone.

Woo's mother was rumored to be able to "put roots on men." She placed such a hold on them—a gift she had never mastered, so it brought her much pain. She never saw any peace, which added to her mental stress. Her mother possessed Oshun energy. She loved men, but she did not desire to be "kept or tied down." It was not in her nature. She had mastered the art of seduction. As the saying went, "They'll fall in love with your freedom then try and cage you." She kept a man until she found a better one, then she was gone without so much as a goodbye with whatever she could throw in a few bags. Her mother was attached to nothing—including her only child.

The next evening, Woo was in lock-up making good on her internal promise to pass out Gatorade. The universe must have taken pity on her for the night before because the shift was going great so far.

Woo nodded her head beside Carter to the music that blasted from his office. Opposite of Idris, whatever floor he worked was as hype as he was. It was so loud they had to yell to communicate to each other. An older trustee swept debris from the cluttered floor. The door that led to Intake opened, and in walked Capone, a buff Italian inmate with ice blue eyes. He walked in escorted by West, a slim, mild mannered, Middle Eastern deputy whose passive ways made easy for the inmates to run all over him.

Capone was returning from his last day of court on a murder charge.

Woo and Carter looked up.

"Well?" they said in unison.

"Not guilty, baby!" Capone threw his hands up and yelled. He would be released.

"Congrats!" Woo shouted, momentarily forgetting she was at work and doing a quick shimmy.

Carter, never passing up an opportunity to turn up, began cheering.

Inmates sent ripped tissue and whatever else they could spare flying like confetti.

Capone was moved to tears.

I just swept this shit up. The trustee shook his head.

"Now you know if his ass was Black, he wouldn't be going nowhere," Carter joked as the door closed behind Capone and West.

"Oh, hell nah," Woo agreed, waving her hand at the thought.

Capone was scheduled for midnight release.

Woo was working through the night and was in booking. Capone, along with Ray, an older Black man in on a probation violation, waited to be processed out.

Truthfully, Woo hadn't gone back upstairs yet in hopes to see Ray off. He was the one who had given her the nickname "lil sis" because he said she looked too young to be there. He'd gotten caught up in the system many years ago, selling drugs while in his twenties. By his thirties he was a heroin addict, and now in his seventies, he'd been clean for over ten years.

Ray had given away all his property earlier that day since he'd no longer need it; he would be staying with his daughter.

Right at midnight, Capone popped his head into the medical booking office.

"All right, lil sis, I'm gone." He smiled.

"Take care of yourself, and don't come back. Where's Ray? Did he leave already?" She rushed out in one breath. She walked out to the desk where Winston, the booking deputy for the night, was working. He was arguing with Ray.

Woo couldn't stand Winston. He was an antagonist who went out of his way to get his coworkers and the inmates in trouble. The inmates called him a bootlicker, and it suited him. He was the biggest snitch in the building, eager to get his coworkers and the inmates written up. He had discovered Ray had a charge in another city and made the call himself to have him transferred and not released, an oversight that would have otherwise gone unnoticed.

"Damn, Winston, that's foul," Woo said softly in disbelief, her voice just above a whisper.

Outside, Capone embraced his wife. He had his old job waiting for him at her father's tow company.

A woman watched from her car parked next to them. She was exhausted after running around all day preparing for her father's anticipated release. She checked the time and glanced at the doors again.

Capone and his wife drove away.

Inside, Ray sat in a cell awaiting his transfer to serve another estimated sixteen months without even being allowed a phone call to let his daughter know he was no longer getting out.

CHAPTER 3

WOO WAS OFF this weekend, her social life nonexistent as of late. Her home was tranquil, a representation of the peace she longed for inside—incense, candles, and order. The decor was bohemian, and lots of African tribal print masks lined the walls, along with pictures of family members most of whom she had never met but she felt a connection to through her grandmother's stories.

Woo's own framed pictures took up a separate wall of their own in the living room from infancy to her teenage years. Her grandmother had loved photos. She'd cherished them and had dusted them faithfully, speaking to them as she did so.

Woo cleaned the brownstone and the inside of the humongous iron cage belonging to Ruby, her twenty-two-year-old cockatoo.

Both the brownstone and Ruby had been left to her by her late grandmother, who had raised her, along with a nice-sized life insurance policy that she had only dipped into once when she upgraded to a new, black 2018 Honda Accord. She didn't care for anything fancy just as long as she never had to be stuck on the side of the road.

Ruby was serene today as she rocked back and forth, humming on her stand. Ruby, who was once a reflection of Woo's grandmother, was now becoming more and more a reflection of her. Parrots could sense energy and, being that they could see more colors in the ultraviolet spectrum, they could literally see your mood.

Woo always took a few deep breaths, calming herself, before she entered into Ruby's space out of respect. Ruby would tilt her head and peer at her with one eye as if reading her on another frequency. When she went through the anger stage of grieving after losing her grandmother, Ruby would pace and screech loud enough to make her ears ring.

Woo's grieving lasted a few short weeks once she reasoned her grandma had been ready to transition on.

A seemingly healthy seventy-five-year-old, her grandmother had declared she was ready to go, gotten her affairs in order, put on her favorite dress, and slicked her long silver braid back neatly. She simply made up her mind, sat in her chair, closed her eyes, and was gone.

Woo understood sadly. Her grandmother had lived her life and was tired.

Ruby was back to her normal self these days, calm and self-sufficient. As long as Woo acknowledged her when she passed by her tree stand and spoiled her with fruits and veggies, she was content. Sometimes she would ramble and coo at something Woo couldn't see. She went in her cage at night and was let out in the morning with free range of the home, though the older she got, the more she spent her days in her window perch or stand.

Before, when it was nice, she would put Ruby on her shoulder and take her outside, but that brought a lot of unwanted attention. Adults were just as bad as kids when it came to wanting to pet Ruby, who was cautious of strangers. The windows were wide open despite the slight breeze, her grandma's voice in her head. *"It ain't clean if you don't air it out."*

The Isley Brothers crooned from the speakers, incense and candles lit in every room except her grandma's, which was left untouched. She was in her own world, buzzed on sativa and smiling for no reason. Her job could drug test at random, which was why she kept a bottle of Niacin and drank water like a fish. It was unlikely Keene would bother, though. She couldn't swear by the Niacin, but it worked for her. The first time she tried it in nursing school, her whole body had turned red, her skin was hot to the touch, and she itched horribly. Afterwards, she learned to take it with a

Benadryl. In a lot of ways, she felt like a hypocrite at work. She passed meds that she would never take or advise herself. She felt you shouldn't have to take another medicine to cope with a side effect from the first. Everyone wanted the quick easy fix. She would talk until blue in the face about the importance of self-care and safer holistic remedies (granted, options were limited in jail), but most would sit uninterested, only caring to hear from the doctor, sometimes flat-out dismissing her. In turn, the doctor dismissed them. He popped in a few times a week and was out the door within a few hours. If the doctor said, "You've got three months to live or take this pill," then the patient didn't question it. Their faith was in the doctor not themselves, she observed. The belief that the body can heal itself as it is designed to was powerful.

While cleaning a wound on an inmate, she'd explained, "You don't question the fact that this wound on your leg will heal. You know and trust it is supposed to and therefore it does. Have that way of thinking with everything else in your body. Where the mind goes, the rest will follow."

She'd gotten into this line of work to be the change she wanted to see, but she was beginning to realize it wasn't as easy as she thought. She had dabbled in reiki healing, and at times she would do this discreetly, sending healing energy to a wound or pain. This worked better when she knew the ailment. Her grandmother, the botanist, had an herb, tea, or ointment for any natural ailment one could think of. She would stare as if she could see inside the body and find the cause. As a child, Woo thought she had x-ray vision and a built-in lie detector because she always knew when Woo was up to something.

Her phone chimed, and a text from Idris appeared on the screen. He'd gotten her number after the pepper spray incident to make sure she got home safe. Her eyes had been red and swollen by the time she got off, but she had made it home. That was a week ago, and they had been texting back and forth ever since. He'd asked her if she wanted to go see a movie.

What am I doing?

Houston's voice played in her ear, telling her not to shit where she ate. Idris was different, though, as cliché as she knew it sounded. He was so composed and in control, and she felt like she'd known him forever or maybe... he had known her forever.

She texted him back that she'd love to. Two hours later, she was standing in her bathroom mirror taming her baby hairs. She sprayed her locs with a water mist infused with essential oils. She wore an *Assata is welcome here* oversized, off-the-shoulder sweatshirt with tattered sleeves, black leggings, and slouchy socks over her shiny Dr. Martens. She was never one for head-to-toe labels.

Her grandma would say, "Who would you be if it all got taken away?"

That rule didn't apply to her gold jewelry, though, as gold hoops lined her ears in addition to the necklaces, bangles, anklets, and toe rings she wore. *Balance.* She smiled at her reflection. There was value in gold. No one could deny that, and she wore three generations of it, most passed on from her mother and grandmother.

She admired the newly reddish tips Houston had recently dyed for her as she pulled her locks up in a huge messy bun that hung lop-sided on her head. Her coffin nails were matte black, and she dabbed Arabian musk on her temples, neck, and wrists. She coined it an aphrodisiac for all the unwanted male attention it brought; she would never again wear it to work, and she laughed at that memory.

However, she learned musk scents ironically were more of an aphrodisiac to the woman wearing them, blending in with their natural scent. Men were actually picking up the sexual energy the woman put out, granted it wasn't directed at them.

She grabbed her large, black boho bag that was covered in revolutionary freedom fighter pins and stickers and tossed her wallet into it just as Idris texted her that he was outside.

A shiny black Ford F-150 pickup hummed out front; she could see it was new. Idris stood on her stoop wearing a navy blue sweatshirt, light blue jeans, a simple gold chain, and watch. His butter Timb boots were laced like he was from the suburbs. She smiled down at them, deciding she'd tell him later. She inhaled the light, fresh scent of his cologne as it mixed nicely with her fragrance.

They began with small talk as he pulled off. She was quieter than usual and surprisingly nervous. He didn't play any music and was fully attentive to her as usual. He told her he had a sister and younger brother—he was the middle child. Her eyes widened curiously, wondering if he had middle child syndrome by chance. She loved secretly analyzing people. He told her his dad was a judge, and his mom was a homemaker.

Woo shook her head at the irony. Such a vast difference from her childhood. Her father had died in prison when she was four years old, having gotten locked up while her mother was pregnant. From what she was told, her parents were not together long. All she knew was he had met her mother and was quickly intrigued. He was turned out by the young woman and did whatever he could to get enough money to impress her. It didn't. There was always a hustler with more. Getting her attention was an easy task; however, keeping it, he found, was another story. He couldn't take the repeated rejection and had confronted Woo's mother and new boyfriend, stabbing the man sixteen times. Woo's mother was four months pregnant at that time, untouched and unfazed. All Woo knew was that her father was found dead a few years later in his cell covered in his own blood, and no explanation was ever given. She'd never met any of his family. They had moved to Florida after his sentencing, but they sent her cards every birthday and holiday.

Her mother was diagnosed as clinically bipolar during a short bid for possession of narcotics. Her grandmother never accepted the Western world diagnosis. *Nobody gets exploited more than Blacks in the medical industry,* she would say, her own mother in the 1940s having been taken from the home, leaving behind her six children after the small town considered she was crazy and unfit. Woo's grandmother, twelve years old at the time, cared for her younger siblings while their father worked. Her great grandmother was said to have been in a teaching hospital and underwent multiple unnecessary tests and surgeries until she died two years later at the age of forty, a shell of herself. She was buried in a nameless grave in the hospital cemetery. *They label what's different, she gone be okay,* her grandmother insisted. *She just at war with herself.*

Her mother wasn't okay, however. She was promiscuous and turned to drugs, using both uppers and downers to find her solace. She began hearing voices, the same voices that told her to try and gouge out her only child's eye at nine months old to rid her of the evil eye she said she saw and leaving a permanent scar just under the left bottom lid. She felt the child was looking into her, reading her thoughts.

Woo's grandmother had no choice but to put her out, chasing her out the door with a broom. She mended the infant's wound at home and from that day on assumed full responsibility for her. Woo wasn't told about this until she was older; she had never bothered to question the scar— she'd always presumed she was just born with it.

Woo's memories of her mother were mostly outlandish. She had just figured the woman was slightly off. Seeing her only in her manic highs when she would show up unannounced with goodies and lavish gifts, excited and childlike, and always with a new boyfriend. The visits stopped altogether when Woo was eleven. The next year, her mother succumbed to the voices at age thirty-four when she got too high and they told her to slit her wrist.

"Damn," was all Idris could say when she told him. He felt guilty for his comfortable life all of sudden.

"My grandmother said when people in Africa or India hear voices, it was believed to be their ancestors and the voices are soft and positive. You know, relative to them, but here ours are violent, yelling, and strange."

"Ours?" Both of his eyebrows went up questionably.

"You know what I mean." She dismissed the remark. "Some places it's not even considered an illness but signals the importance of the individual, for they are able to communicate in two realms. But sickness, violence, and mental illness are just so common here. You can't tell me the Western world isn't cursed.

"My people have roots in Ghana, and it was always my grandmother's dream to return, but she never made it. I like to think she finally made it there." She exhaled as if the words had been pent up, waiting for someone she could pour them out to, and she now looked relieved and lighter in a sense.

Did the quiet always hold in so much that the words became heavy? He wondered as he stared, silently listening.

"I still got some family here; we just scattered. One of my great aunts calls every time she sees something crazy on the news out this way to see if I came across the person at work." She laughed to ease the seriousness. She concluded, deciding she had said enough for now.

After the movie, the temp had dropped a bit. Idris put his arm around her and pulled her into his side.

"What you think of the movie?" he asked, noticing her demeanor had changed.

"I mean, I thought it was Black empowerment, then at the end in comes the White savior. Kinda threw me off." She shook her head, annoyed.

"Come on. He should've kept quiet and listened when he got pulled over," Idris said.

"Why should we have to reassure them when they're the ones holding the gun? Why should we always have to be uncomfortable for their comfort?" Woo raised her eyebrows, but Idris stayed quiet. "They just need to abolish the police shit," she said angrily.

"Whoa, you mean reform," he said, surprised at her.

"Nope. Did we say reform slavery? No, it had to go. We now have more incarcerated than there were slaves, Idris! So no, I doubt it can be reformed." She crossed her arms, challenging him.

"Fuck our jobs then, huh?" He pushed her as they laughed, the tension broken.

"I'm sure we could find new ones with all the new outreach programs they could fund after putting that money back in the community." She playfully pushed him back.

They went to get something to eat from a lowkey spot that had the best crab cakes around. It was a hidden gem that usually did open mic nights on the weekends.

Woo had piles of poetry books stacked in her room that she had never worked up the courage to share, so she truly admired those who did. She was surprised when Idris suggested this place, but she agreed.

This wasn't just any random spot. Woo and her ex, Khalil, used to frequent here weekly. They had grown up on the same block and were high school sweethearts, born on the same day.

Not long after their engagement, he confessed he had a two-month-old son. From the picture he showed her, the baby looked just like him and was his junior. He made no excuses but was apologetic. The trust was gone, though. As much as she wished she could say she had left him right then, that would be a lie. Not until after months of him leaving for doctors' appointments and whenever something came up for the baby. Out of nowhere she was debunked from first to third. Khalil felt she'd have a change of heart when she met the baby, and she did. A surge of emotions came over her—love, betrayal, and jealousy were a few. She knew then that it wouldn't work. The next day she changed her number and ignored his attempts to get her back. That was three years ago, and now here he was.

He'd shaved the sides of his locks that otherwise were the same length as hers pulled back in a low ponytail, and he now had a beard, which matured him nicely. Khalil had coffee brown skin and piercing almond eyes. He had sharp features and a presence that demanded attention. He was still the most handsome man she had ever seen. He was wearing a gold ankh necklace, and her hand absentmindedly grazed the tattoo that matched it on her right wrist.

Their eyes met, and she looked away quickly, her heart now racing.

Idris, who never missed a detail, looked toward her distraction. He slid closer to her and placed his hand over hers just as Khalil approached.

"Good evening, y'all. Willow, it's been a long time," he said, looking her over subtly. She'd filled out nicely, but he knew that. He had never stopped keeping tabs on her, though he respected her wishes and left her alone. It'd be rude not to speak now, though, since she was here, he reasoned.

Idris took a sip of his drink, remaining silent.

"Yes, it has, uh... this is my friend, Damien," she said. It was her first time calling Idris by his first name, and it felt awkward.

"I just wanted to speak. Don't be a stranger." Khalil nodded, put off by the sinister look in the other man's eyes, and he walked away before she could respond.

Idris was still staring.

"That was my ex," was all she said before biting into her crab cake.

A few nights later, work was pure chaos. Day shift had been giving flu shots all week for the ones who didn't refuse, and before Woo could set her bag down, she was getting back-to-back calls concerning inmates.

"Now if this ain't reason enough not to get that shit, I don't know what is. It's hundreds of strains of the flu. What are the odds they got it right with the exact immunization for this flu season?" Woo said to Carter, who was the medical deputy that night.

As usual, he could care less.

"Them niggas 'bout to die?" he joked.

Woo's head jerked up as she looked around before whispering, "Never call on death, it will eventually answer."

She rushed over to knock on the nearest table just in case.

"Never make fun of anyone unless you ready to switch places with them." She waved her finger at him.

"Here you go with that voodoo shit you be talking," he said as he nudged her.

"Well, what did your ancestors do before White America told them it was evil? Hell, we didn't know evil til they told us we were," she countered.

"True." He shrugged, knowing if he objected, she would go on and on about the subject.

They eventually had to create a separate pod for the sick inmates in an attempt to contain the virus.

The two approached the pod and, as her grandmother would say, "You could smell the sick."

It was a sad sight to see grown men so pitiful.

"They killing y'all!" Wade yelled out. He was an outspoken, older, light-skinned man who read all day and hollered all night. Most wrote him off as crazy due to his disheveled appearance.

Woo listened to him when she wasn't in a rush, even if they disagreed on a subject.

Even a broken clock is right twice a day, she figured.

"They doing y'all like my buddies at Killer King Hospital! Lil sis, you know better than to be injecting that poison!" he yelled.

"I didn't give no flu shots," she said defensively.

"You would if they told you," he silenced her. "Medical warfare! Prison warfare!" he sang, banging his cup against the bars.

"Calm down, old head," Carter said.

Wade, ironically, was born in prison. According to him, his parents were locked up together at a time and place where males and females weren't kept separate. He was auctioned off when he turned six years old right out front that prison as if he were a puppy in the pound. That's as far as he told his story, the rest assumed too painful because he would never speak of it. Perhaps buried in the place memories too much to bear disappear to.

Woo knew of that all too well.

He refused all medical and mental health treatment but had a bad heroin addiction on the outside.

Woo maintained a soft spot for him. A number of males that came in ended up getting placed on psychiatric meds they didn't need but abused to get some sleep, which was the reason a lot of them now had full breasts, an irreversible side effect, and some even leaked.

After the exhausting ordeal, Woo lounged in the breakroom with Carter and Houston. Houston was knocked out, snoring lightly, on the couch beside Carter. Her feet rested on his knees, but he didn't move them.

"So what's that mean?" Carter nodded toward her ankh tattoo.

"It represents the male and female genitalia—that which brings forth life." She smiled to lessen the seriousness she felt when she spoke, a habit she always did. "See, the way I see it, God is a woman, being that only women can bring forth life from the spiritual plane, so the womb is the universe."

Carter shrugged, so she continued.

"Anyway, back to the ankh, if she so mighty who would she create with...but herself, possessing both male and female parts because you must be complete to be whole; and if she's all-knowing and all-seeing, how can she not be whole? Some say that's why we pray on our knees, bringing us eye level to worship the womb which we came from. Of course, this belief was lost when patriarchy was brought to Africa by the White man claiming to want to save the very same souls that he colonized, raped, and trafficked. Yet he calls us savages."

Carter just smiled and shook his head.

Woo's phone rang, catching her off guard. It was 2:00 a.m.

"Saved by the bell," he joked.

"Shut the hell up." She playfully put up her middle finger. She was mostly quiet, so at times she talked in waves, words pouring out.

It was Idris calling. He was off tonight. Cellphones were forbidden on the secure side of the jail. *How the hell does he know I have my phone?* She sent the call to voicemail.

Carter's phone chimed.

"What the fuck." His face scrunched up. "It's ya boy." He held his phone up to Woo's face.

"Yo! What's good? Work busy?"

"I ain't even know he still had my number." He looked at Woo for a second, genuinely confused. She put her hands up, shrugging. They silently dismissed the subject.

After a few more minutes, she stood, stretched, and gently shook Houston awake.

"Time to clock back in."

The three placed their phones in their respective lockers and went back into Medical.

Later that morning, Woo was so sleepy she didn't know how she made it home. Turner was over an hour and a half late to relieve her and had the audacity to have an attitude when she came in.

Woo pulled up to her brownstone. *I must be hallucinating.* She blinked, but still Idris's truck was parked out front. She refused to look his way as she went inside and locked the door. She had no clue how to process this right now.

She peeled her scrubs off as she walked straight into the bathroom. She got into the shower and turned the water on as hot as she could take, her phone on the sink buzzing the whole time.

It was still vibrating when she got out.

"Hello," she answered dryly.

"Hey, I was just checking on you. You never called me back," he said in almost a whining tone.

She remained silent on the other end of the phone.

"Look, I just wanted to make sure you ate. I left breakfast at the door. I'm gone," he said.

She softened as she opened the door in her sleep kaftan and retrieved the bag of takeout. His truck was gone.

"I appreciate breakfast, but I gotta go, I'm real tired," she told him.

"Yeah, I bet you and your boy had a long night. Get some rest."

The call ended. *What the hell?* She stared at the phone in her hand. She didn't like this possessive side of him that she was seeing more and more of.

Everybody know Carter ain't shit, he had warned her not long ago. She had asked him what that had to do with her, being that she and Carter were just cool. Funny thing was Carter had already told her that much.

I may not be shit as a CO, son, brother, friend, whatever, but nobody can say I'm a bad father, he told her, speaking of his three-year-old son.

And you get a treat for that, she told him, dropping two Starbursts in his hand, laughing. Didn't make a difference to her.

Too exhausted to eat, she set the food in the microwave and collapsed on top of her covers.

CHAPTER 4

IDRIS HAD WARNED her it would be a busy night because the police department was doing a warrant sweep. That meant they would have a whole lot of new intakes.

Operation hammer all over again. Woo sadly scanned the room. Booking was a madhouse, cells were full, and people were standing. About 95 percent of the new intakes were Black.

Guess White folks don't have no warrants.

Idris told her a few weeks ago the sheriff was in plans to build a new jail. At first, that sounded like a good idea since this one was falling apart. The water was so harsh that her hands burned and broke out in blisters with nonstop itching and peeling until she brought a jug from home to wash them with while at work.

Unfortunately, the inmates continued to suffer with dry skin and rashes. One literally had skin falling off his back. She had wrapped and treated it as a wound for weeks until he got out.

She thought it would be a good idea until she found out this new jail would be three times bigger. Who would fill it? Funding for a new jail also meant proving the current one was overpopulated. Idris never told her how he knew before anyone else. Or how he always had the drop on everything before it happened.

Houston was coming down to give her a break. She leaned against the wall to wait beside the magistrate's office as a young White cop went in to discuss the White girl he'd just brought in on a DUI.

The magistrate, an older White man, appeared on a screen via video chat.

"Two questions," he rushed. "What's her race and did she cooperate?" he asked.

Woo's head popped up.

The cop cleared his throat.

"White and yes, she's very remorseful," he said.

"Sounds easy enough, bring her in," the magistrate told him.

Houston walked up.

"You good?" she asked.

Woo dropped the office keys in her hand.

"Yeah, just gotta get the fuck from down here."

Woo was working overnight with Houston, who was on the phone with her new boyfriend.

The deputies were bringing down someone for a fight.

Woo smiled when she looked up at Cleveland being escorted in. The two got along great and made jokes about the red incident as well as the pepper spray which she playfully blamed him for. She just happened to be wearing a royal blue scrub set.

"Oh, so you knew I was coming? Looking like a blueberry," he laughed. She checked his vitals before he was taken to Isolation. Isolation was a world of its own. She'd been in an iso cell for about fifteen minutes when a code was called on an unconscious inmate who'd tried to drown himself in the toilet, and she'd felt like the walls were closing in on her.

"Stay strong, Cle!" Houston called from the nurses' station, raising a fist in the air just before the door closed. "That's a real one right there." She aimed a pointed nail at the now closed door before she picked the phone back up.

Shortly after Cleveland left, the fourth floor called. There was a big incident in 4D, and some inmates needed to come down. The pod was mostly young boys, and for the past few weeks a number of them had come down to be treated for the same STD even though none were fresh off the street. Throughout the day, they got in trouble for making curtains out of their sheets and walking around in only boxers.

One they brought down was a fifty-year-old autistic man named Wolfe. West was holding him up. One of his eyes was swollen shut, and he'd been beaten pretty badly.

Woo and Houston worked together to get him cleaned up. When they asked him what happened, Wolfe kept repeating, "I wrote the social worker and Lt, told them to get me outta there!"

"Why was he in there with all them young boys anyway?" Houston slammed the peroxide down and looked around the room as if for the answer.

West shrugged, not wanting to say anything and get yelled at. They seemed mad.

Wolfe was moved to lock-up where he could be monitored; it was clear he wasn't the aggressor. The last to come down was Parker, the ringleader in that pod.

Woo couldn't stand Parker. He was obnoxious and disrespectful. He'd been in a lock-up cell with Wade while Woo was doing rounds, and Wade was yelling as usual. Parker had asked Woo for a cup of her water, which he used to dump on Wade.

"You better not ever ask me for shit else," she had hissed at him, repulsed.

"Where you hurt?" she asked, looking him up and down for any injuries.

Parker stood and dropped his boxers. He pulled back the foreskin on his penis, revealing a bite mark.

"What the hell?" Houston leaned back.

"Man, I was beating dude ass, then he fell and sat up to bite me!" he yelled animatedly.

"Wait... You would've had to been hard. What was y'all doing to him?" It was a rhetorical question because she was already making her own conclusion.

"You accusing me of doin' gay shit? Fuck that!" Parker yelled.

"Umm, your wound don't add up with your story," Woo said, unfazed.

He pushed the wound cart over, and West called for assistance over the radio.

"Nasty ass," Woo fussed as Parker was dragged out.

"Girl, he not circumcised; he was putting his dick in Wolfe mouth, I'm glad he bit that shit!" She put her hands on her hips and fumed.

"Damn," Houston said as she logged on to her Facebook.

It was almost time for her shift to be over when a short young man with medium brown skin stumbled into the booking office.

Her eyes zeroed in on his poorly wrapped, bandaged upper arm; the dressing was soiled with dried blood. She hopped up and put on her gloves, already walking toward him.

"When did this happen?"

He looked up.

"Uh, two days ago." He wiped sweat from his brow.

Woo cut the old bandage and cleaned and rewrapped the gunshot wound which went in through the front and out the back. The wound didn't appear infected, yet he was sweating in a cold room.

"You taking anything?" she asked, putting the thermometer under his tongue for him since one arm was bad, and his other hand wasn't in much better shape.

"Uhh... my girl got my meds, but I ain't took nothing yet."

His temp was 103, so she administered some Tylenol to bring it down and called the doctor.

"He needs something stronger for pain, and his temp is elevated, so I think he needs to go out to the hospital to rule out infection."

She held her breath, awaiting his response. He was a horrible doctor with racist ways and never took their concerns seriously.

"Well, if he hasn't been taking his meds, why should we give him any?" he said smugly.

"Well, since he is in our care, we should." She couldn't mask the irritation in her voice as she glanced at the man sitting before her, offering him a reassuring smile.

The doctor yawned loudly in her ear and rambled off an order for antibiotics and Tylenol 3.

"Thanks." She slammed the phone down before he could say something slick. She put the man on fifteen minute checks after giving him his meds and rechecking his temp.

"Make sure you remember my guy," she passed on in report before she left.

CHAPTER 5

IDRIS HAD BEEN pulled to dayshift the past few days due to them being so short staffed.

Woo had been distant toward him since the day he was outside her house, but she was starting to miss him. He was back on nights now and was escorting her as she did detox on the eighth floor. They approached 8D where Bandi, Cleveland's cousin and their most notorious inmate at the time, was housed. He was awaiting trial for murder and kingpin charges.

"My favorite nurse." Bandi openly eyed her. "What's the math?" he joked, nodding toward her neck tattoo.

She smiled.

"I need to see my detoxers." She awaited his response. Nobody was gonna come up until he moved or gave the okay anyway.

"Ay Id, you move that shit yet?" he asked seriously. Her detoxers could wait.

"Yeah, I got that trash out," Idris said in a hushed tone, narrowing his eyes at Bandi for asking him that in front of Woo.

What the hell did he move? She looked away quickly as if she hadn't heard a thing.

They walked the long hall after she finished detox and as they approached the office, he gently pulled her inside by the elbow.

"You mad at me or something?" He raised her chin to meet his intense gaze.

"Not mad, just don't need nobody keeping tabs on me." She exhaled, relieved to get that off her chest.

The sound of keys jingling got closer. They stepped apart just as Lt. Flores, a middle-aged White woman with a Northern accent, stopped at the door. She paused to wipe the sweat from her brow and catch her breath; she looked red and clammy. She was heavyset but seemed to be losing weight dramatically. She looked Woo up and down.

"Distracting my deputies as usual?" She smirked. "Your deputies?" Woo parroted, hoping she could hear how ridiculous her statement was.

Flores was always saying something shady to her or overstepping her bounds in Medical. All Woo knew was something wasn't right with her.

"I'm out," she told Idris as she passed Flores without acknowledgement.

Mack was fussing to herself when Woo got back into Medical. One of the inmates from her med pass got moved to the eighth floor before she got to them.

"Want me to take it? I just left from up there." Woo held her hand out for the med cup.

"I got it. I do everything round here anyhow. What's one more thing?" Mack shook her head.

That's a damn lie. Woo chuckled.

"Who working the eighth floor?" Mack questioned.

"Idris." *She 'bout to say something smart.* Woo raised her eyebrows expectantly.

"Great. Slow boy." Mack rolled her eyes.

Woo laughed as Mack walked out, mumbling to herself.

It was 4:00 a.m., and Woo and Mack were both knocked out at the nurses' station.

A screeching sound over the speakers jolted them awake.

"Jesus!" Mack dramatically clutched her chest.

Woo sat attempting to rub away the sleep lines as she looked around, disoriented.

"You smell smoke?" she asked once she recognized the sound as the fire alarm.

Winston ran in.

"Civilians! Exit the building now!" he shouted though they were right in front of him.

"Is it a fire?" Mack asked. It was cold and rainy outside.

Winston put his hand up.

"Just a minute, ma'am. Deputy Winston reporting from Medical, instructing medical personnel to exit the premises."

Who the hell is he even talking to? Nobody ever responds to his radio traffic with his silly ass.

"Ladies, I need you to pick it up!" a deep voice boomed from the doorway.

"What the fuck you doing in here? Go secure your floor!" Idris ordered as he stepped face to face with Winston.

Winston pushed his glasses up with his finger and left hurriedly in silence.

"So is it a fire or not?" Mack repeated, irritated, standing with her arms crossed.

"Nah, just somebody smoking weed, and they can't get the alarm to shut off." He was calm Idris again.

Woo, now fully awake and curious, spoke up.

"If it was a real fire, where do the inmates go?"

"Nowhere," he said somberly.

Once he was gone, Mack started in on him.

"He ain't never far, now, is he?"

"Seems that way," Woo admitted as the realization froze her.

"Couldn't be me. Nope, I don't need no man loving me to death." Mack shook her head. Her words sent a chill down Woo's back as she knocked on the table.

After work, she and Idris sat close at a small breakfast diner.

"I'm just saying, the bitch always lurking, like she watching me. Let me know if I'm tripping. I don't know," she shrugged, speaking of Flores.

"She might like you." Idris stuck his tongue out at her playfully. His hand dropped to her thigh, and she recoiled at the unexpected touch. He'd noticed many times how jumpy she was and then at times she seemed to operate in a tranquil state. He couldn't figure her out, but he was working on it.

They discussed work some more.

"So this lady mom is blowing up the phone, begging to get us to sneak her daughter breastmilk to her. I told her it's unethical and against policy to, and come to find out, the mom has drugs in her system, and the baby was withdrawing from not having them. On top of that, the grandma knew." She shook her head.

"Damn shame," Idris responded. He sometimes lacked empathy.

She wished she could give him some of hers so she wouldn't have to hold in so much. When it was time to pay, he turned to conceal the thick wad of cash.

She acted like she got a notification on her phone, but she hadn't missed it.

"Aye, you know if you ever need anything, I got you, right?" He looked her in the eye seriously.

"Noted." She stretched. "All I need now, though, is some sleep."

She pulled into the parking lot at work. She had to get her mind right before going in. She envied her coworkers who she watched pull up and just casually hop out of their cars, no mental prep needed. That was never the case with her. She had to brace herself.

When she got inside, Keene was waiting for her. She sat in his cluttered office as he coughed and spit in his trash can. She turned away in disgust. She was a nurse, but the sight of spit made her stomach turn, and that cough sounded like he had one foot in the grave and the other on a banana peel.

Damn Turner, how? She shuddered, picturing them together.

Keene cleared his throat, bringing her out of her thoughts.

"It seems Parker is not too happy with you at the moment," he said. "The deputies heard him on a recorded call... Let's just say he was making plans for you."

Parker blamed her for word getting out about the Wolfe incident.

"Everybody knew, though," Woo said as she adjusted her lab jacket over her thighs, which appeared double the size spread in the small chair, accidentally knocking over her tote bag. Her used copy of Malcolm X's autobiography spilled to the floor.

Keene's eyes squinted as he read the cover.

"That's not for an inmate, is it?"

She shook her head. "It's mine," she answered.

"Well, keep it on the unsecure side. Those types of books are banned here."

"What type may that be?" She leaned forward, squinting her eyes back at him. She had an odd habit of mocking gestures when conversing with people. She had no idea why and a lot of times wasn't aware she did it.

"You know. Divisive. Could get the inmates riled up if they get their hands on something like that. Anyhow, for your safety, he's being transferred, but you should get an order of protection since he only has a few weeks left," Keene advised.

"I'll be careful." She stood, eager to get out of the cramped office, shutting the door behind her.

Waiting on the other side of the door was Barr. Woo tolerated but didn't trust her. She was part time, but whenever she came to work, drama followed. That in itself was baffling with all she had going on outside of work. They got multiple phone calls from disgruntled girlfriends trying to catch up with her.

Black girl lost.

"Why were you in there?" Barr asked as if she wasn't eavesdropping.

"Nothing." Woo brushed by her. She was always trying to find out stuff to later use to her advantage, most likely as leverage. Barr had been written up for fraternizing with the inmates on more than one occasion from the security side. She stood there now, spilling out of her tight scrubs in all the wrong places.

Not today. Woo smiled at her. Whatever she did would catch up to her. Woo wasn't worried.

CHAPTER 6

WOO WAS OFF work and had stopped in a Black-owned bookstore she frequented. It had been a few months since she'd read a good book. She low-key wanted to annoy Keene with another book; he was always commenting on her reading material now.

Her brownstone was filled with books stacked high in rows along the wall, on the tables, lined in the windows, and used as plant stands. She could thank her grandmother for that. There was no cable or internet in her home growing up. She gave in and got both while she was in nursing school.

She wore an Angela Davis tee, Nomad sweatpants, espadrilles, and a long, hooded cardigan with frayed sleeves. Her nails were blood red, her power color. Her locs were pulled back from her face, three on each side, looped in a knot, the rest in the back hanging loose. Her red reading glasses, she hoped, hid her lower than normal eyes from her morning wake and bake.

"Willow," a low voice called to her.

She looked up from the book she was skimming to see Khalil.

"Salam." He nodded.

"Wa alaikum salam." She nodded as she pressed her palms together, smiling. He looked good as usual, a fresh line up and re-twist, wearing all black, with Malcolm X glasses.

"Your man not with you today?" He hoped she would say that was just her friend.

"Just me," she answered vaguely.

Once the ice was broken, conversation flowed for the once lovers. They sat cross-legged on the carpet catching up. He showed her pictures of his little boy, who was adorable, and cracked her up with stories of how mischievous he was.

"Like father, like son," she said, reminiscing on how much trouble Khalil used to stay in.

He was still working as an electrician and doing activist work, but not as much as he'd like.

"I still worry about you. You sure you okay?" he asked seriously.

"I'm not trying to revisit that." She knew he would go there. Most likely speaking on one of the mental breakdowns he'd witnessed when she was in nursing school. The fast-paced program had nearly driven her crazy. She looked like she was doing just fine, but he knew her better than anyone else.

It was the inside he was worried about. They exchanged numbers as they exited the bookstore two hours later.

Woo gasped when she got close to her black Honda Accord—her two driver's side tires were slashed.

"Damn, who you make mad?" Khalil approached her side.

She peered inside the windows and glanced around before she answered.

"Most likely an inmate who just got out." She thought of Parker and rolled her eyes.

"Come on." Khalil led her to his car as he made arrangements to have hers towed. They sat together at the tire shop.

"You got any kind of protection?" he asked.

"Umm, pepper spray and a switchblade," she said.

"Still?" He chuckled as she nodded.

"Well, it's a new blade now." She smiled slyly. "This is bullshit though. I don't bother nobody," she pouted. She refused his offer to follow her home once the car was done.

"Aye, no matter what time it is call me if you need me. I'ma let you hold on to my gun too for as long as you need it," he said sincerely.

"You don't have to do that," she said.

"I do. We as a people used to look out for our own and feel safe among each other, not tear each other down." He sighed, staring off.

"I'll let you know." She hugged him tightly before she left.

Later that night, Ruby was squealing followed by a loud slam. The shrill of her scream was deafening, unlike her usual whistle, chirp, or song.

Woo sat up in bed, the urgency in Ruby's scream making her heart pound. She picked up her cell phone and squinted her eyes to adjust to the brightness. *1:44*. Her hands trembled as she stumbled, disoriented, toward Ruby's cage in the darkness.

"Shhh, it's okay, Ruby, hush," she whispered through the tattered, thin throw blanket that hung over the cage every night. Her phone rang. It was Idris.

"I think somebody threw something at my front window," she blurted out.

"I'm out front. Open the door," he ordered.

She peeked through the peephole and there he stood in an athletic gray sweatsuit. She hadn't been so happy to see someone in a long time. She opened the door and squeezed him tight. She inhaled his everyday scent mixed with light sweat and alcohol.

"What were you even doing out here?" she asked once the door was shut and locked.

"I went and got a few drinks with a couple of friends and decided to drive past on my way home. Good thing I did cas I saw a dark car speed off." He showed her the brick he'd picked up from out front.

"Why did you bring that in here? Should I call and report it?" she asked.

"Nah, it's probably Parker. But don't worry. I can get to him better than the police can," he assured her.

She led him into her bedroom, grateful she wasn't alone tonight. She told him about her tire incident from earlier, leaving out Khalil's involvement.

"You should've called me," he said, nuzzling his face into her locs as he cradled her from behind. "I told you I got you."

She pulled away from him, reached down, and came up with a colorful ashtray, plucking out a blunt left behind from that morning. They'd just made gentle love for the first time, and her mind was racing.

"Why you smoke that shit?" he asked.

"It's just weed." She inhaled. "Organic, au natural." She giggled as the weed took effect. "I need it; it keeps me balanced," she said seriously.

"Tell me why." He sat up with her.

"I think I have PTSD and stints of paranoia to where... sometimes I look back and don't know if what I'm experiencing is real or all in my head. I was raped... by my best friend at the time's older brother. It was nighttime and she was asleep, at least she acted like she was. Kinda why I don't really have friends now." She paused as she recalled the terror. "I still have nightmares. I fear it's gonna push me over the edge. I try to get so high that when I go to sleep my spirit leaves my body and I just soar so I won't have to dream. At the end of the day, I just don't wanna end up like my mom," she confessed.

"So where's he now?" Idris asked. He didn't care how long ago it was; he wanted to make him pay.

She looked over to him.

"Oh, he's dead," she said coldly, the glare from the lit blunt casting an unsettling glow on the smile that slowly spread across her face.

CHAPTER 7

IDRIS HAD BEEN chosen to work on the special task force at work, which meant more hours. There had been an increase of contraband in the jail.

The week before, an inmate had overdosed and had to be Narcaned. He was alive but was in the hospital in critical care. The sheriff was cracking down on security measures.

Woo was doing med pass with Carter at 8D.

"God is good," Bandi greeted her.

"Why's that?" Woo said, surprised by his upbeat demeanor.

"Well, my homeboy died today, and I just found out," Bandi told her, smiling.

"And... we're happy?" she asked, confused.

"Yeah, he was a snitch. But we gone still get who got him anyway," he assured her.

"Okay, cool." She shrugged. *Whatever.*

"Aye, Carter, I need you to get something for me," he said, his tough persona returning.

"Hell, nah," Carter said.

"I wasn't asking you." Bandi narrowed his eyes.

"What you gone do? Shoot me?" Carter shrugged.

Woo laughed outright, and even Bandi had to chuckle.

"You lucky I like you, man." He walked away to hide his amusement.

Downstairs, she waited for control to open the door for the last med pass of her shift.

"Ah hell." She shook her head as she stepped in. The inmates were out on rec *finally,* and their cells were being tossed.

"What y'all doing?" Woo asked one of the newer deputies in training.

"Looking for contraband," the young White boy said, not looking up.

"Damn," she said to herself. Belongings were everywhere. She steered her cart through the debris and did med pass out on the yard, feeling bad for the unsuspecting men who were just happy to get some air. No doubt they were gonna flip when they got back in. *Let me get my ass back upstairs before shit hits the fan.*

Outside of work, Woo had been feeling strange lately, like someone was following and watching her. Her nightmares had returned more vivid than ever. Someone was killing her, and she couldn't move, speak, or see their face. She felt herself spiraling mentally. She hadn't told Idris.

He took being there for her as the job of being her personal bodyguard.

He was surprised when he caught her mumbling and talking to herself a few times. She'd told him she just needed rest. She needed alone time to take the mask off. Instead, she called Khalil. He understood her and wouldn't crowd. He met up with her at the gun range. He wanted her to brush up on her skills before he handed his gun over to her.

The whole time he drove her crazy with his rules, reminders, and tips. She'd forgotten how bossy he could be. He stood behind her, adjusting her stance and holding on to the gun. She acted more annoyed than she was, enjoying their reunion.

Inside the gun range, he held her tight. When they finished, he walked her to her car. He leaned in the window and placed the gun and a black bag into her lap.

"You not still hearing them voices, are you?" he asked her, concerned. He wanted her to have the gun for protection but would hate himself if she ended up doing something crazy with it. He dismissed the thought when she looked down, embarrassed.

She hated to talk about it, but Khalil knew. He was there. She had pushed him away so much in that time she reasoned that was why he stepped out on her. She wouldn't excuse it, though.

"I know how to silence them," she half told the truth. They said goodbye, and she allowed him to lean in and kiss her on the lips. He stood and waited until she pulled out of the parking lot.

Khalil had been running all day after leaving Woo; he hadn't even had time to text her. He had to take his lil man to the ER for a double ear infection. He'd just pulled in his driveway, coming from dropping the child off to his mother.

He smiled, thinking about his morning with Willow. He would've been there either way, but he hoped this would lead to something. She was his first love, and getting her back finally seemed like a reality.

He opened his door, but before getting out, remembered how his son always trashed his backseat.

He hated to leave junk in his beloved car overnight. It was a black-on-black X5 that he kept in pristine condition. He leaned back to grab whatever was left behind. He thought he heard footsteps as he turned back toward the front with a handful of happy meal trash. He looked up to see a shadowy figure standing over him. He reached under his seat, feeling around for what was no longer there.

"Shit." The last thing he saw was a set of evil eyes, one with a silver streak, gleaming before he heard the loud pop.

CHAPTER 8

IT HAD BEEN a week since Khalil's death. Woo was devastated. Here she was with his gun for safety, and he had been killed because he hadn't had it.

She folded the cut-out of his obituary and set it on top of her ancestral altar along with a picture she had of him. There had only been a brief mention of his murder on the news, and there were no suspects. They'd alluded to a robbery gone too far. She couldn't imagine what his mother and son were going through. His gun was under her mattress, and the bag he'd given her sat unopened on top of her dresser.

Woo was back at work which, surprisingly, ended up being a much-needed distraction. On top of everything else, Idris was draining her. He picked arguments over how she chose to grieve Khalil's death, not liking that the attention was not on him during this time.

She was in the control room watching cameras with Carter, cracking up at the inmates' and even coworkers' antics they witnessed.

Barr sashayed away from a cell of her rumored inmate lover.

"You know she mad at me, right?" Carter told her. A few months ago, Barr was talking slick about her in the presence of inmates while on med pass with Carter. He spoke to her simply and told her it wasn't cool.

"Jealous ho." Woo rolled her eyes. "She ain't think "She ain't think I was gonna tell you. Of course I'ma tell you, you my nigga" he grinned at her. "Oh look, there go boo" he pointed to Idris as appeared on the screen. They quieted as they watched Idris walk over and retrieve something from the trash can on the 8th floor. He shoved it in his pocket and disappeared in his office, he emerged seconds later with a brown snack bag. *Nobody in that pod is assigned a snack bag.* Sometimes deputies bartered with them or gave them to inmates who were helpful she reasoned. He strolled over to 8D where Bandi was waiting, Idris passed the bag to him. Carter turned his attention to a pod of young boys horse playing "look at these dummies" he laughed. "Wait, what just happened?" Woo still fixated on Idris. "Oh that, them niggas been doing that shit. I know everything that comes in here and who brings it in" he dismissed like it was nothing waving his hand. "You knew and didn't tell me!" she squealed. "Thought you knew" he shrugged.

As soon as she was back in medical a code went off location 8D. She grabbed the emergency bag and took of fas fast as she could although the thing was almost as big as he. She caught her breath on the elevator ride up with a laid black acorn skin deputy named Cobb. Once in the pod there passed out in the stall beside the toilet was Pierre drenched in sweat. Normally anyone else would be fair game but Pierre ran this pod. Originally from Haiti he was in on a murder charge, he had snapped and killed his wife for "one day she wouldn't shut up" he admittedly stated. One glance she could see his belly was distended and at touch it was as hard as a rock. He had come down a few times for constipation all he'd been given was magnesium citrate until he was caught trying to smuggle a bottle back upstairs. They wheeled him down on a makeshift gurney to the clinic. He was now conscious and clutching his stomach moaning. The impacted bowel was visible after he followed instruction to lay on his side with one leg up. "Now this won't be fun for either of us but I have to disimpact you" she double gloved up. "As you will" he moaned. The smell was rancid as she reached in broke off a chunk of BM and dumped it in the pail propped underneath him. They stood no chance in the stuffy clinic. Cobbs leaned against the wall as he watched in disbelief as the small nurse pulled chunk after chunk from the huge man. Finally enough leeway was made for him to do the rest on the toilet. Pierre walked out in instant relief with a new respect for the young nurse they shared a quick smile as he passed with a much smaller stomach. She turned away as so he wouldn't get the wrong idea after learning the hard way a simple prolonged smile could be too easily mistaken for a love connection.

A week later she was over Idris apartment, she opted to spend time there so she could leave at her will and go home to enjoy solitude. He had a very nice apartment too *he did say his father was a judge though.* She never mentioned what she saw on the cameras and had chosen not to judge. Although she wanted to warn him it may not be as under wraps as he thought, whatever he was doing.

They laughed and joked at last nights work drama where their usual 3 prostitutes came into booking none of which were under 65 years old. They were always hilarious when they came in albeit the whole situation was sad. The oldest one Miss Shelia at 73 drunkenly exposed her relationship with deputy Clark. She said he had given her a ride after her last release which was forbidden then got oral sex in his car. She was scorned he didn't pay her. She was telling all his personal business as well. Woo was disturbed since Miss Sheila was HIV positive and Clark young enough to be her grandson had a girlfriend at home. Clark was already accepted into the police academy and was allowed to resign quietly.

Idris hung up his phone, "I gotta go in" he said." "Everything okay?" she sat up. She was comfortable at the moment, one thing about Idris he catered to her if she was coming over he went out of his way to provide her every need so she wouldn't have a reason to leave, she had even gained 5 lbs messing with him. But she did need to get home to tend to Ruby. "Bandi got caught with some shit and the higher ups called a meeting" he told her. She tried to read him by his tone but was unable, he was unreadable, usually people like that had something to hide. "I made you a key in case you wanna chill here and I'm out" he tossed a silver key at her, she didn't catch it so it landed beside her. She didn't feel comfortable having it. "I'm going out after you but I'll hold on to it... in case I need it" she said.

She came into work later that night and went straight to Idris floor. Lt Flores was walking out office in a huff. *Oh shit, I should've called up here first.* Flores walked past her in silence for once. Woo was thinking Idris had gotten in trouble and rushed in. "What happened?" she caught her breath. He was leaning against his desk, his forehead wrinkled he slowly looked at her. "Bandi got put in isolation for now" he wiped his brow. "Everything gonna be okay?" she asked. "If not, I'ma make it okay" he told her coldly.

Ever since Bandi had got in trouble she had been walking on eggshells. Idris was showing up unannounced, demanding her whereabouts and calling her phone over and over. She'd finally told him she needed space. She avoided him at work where he would never make a scene at work but outside was a different story. She had just pulled up at home and his truck was parked right out front her home. "Shit, not again" she mumbled when he got out the same time she did. She was pissed but didn't want her nosey neighbors to start looking out their windows not that they would bother to help. He walked in on the back of her heels pushing her in the back before she could turn and close the door. "What the fuck! You can't just bust up in here!" she yelled. "It's Carter huh" he answered himself "yeah it is, I been knew that" he nodded. "You're crazy" she pushed him back. "You trying to get him killed too" he sneered. She stumbled back, she felt dizzy and sick. He grabbed her by the wrist as she slid down the wall unable to hold herself up. He dragged her back up to her feet, using one hand to hold her hands down while the other squeezed her neck. She froze what he'd just told her disabled her fight or flight and she couldn't move. He leaned down and whispered in her ear "if you care about that nigga stay away from him" he turned her loose roughly. He then picked up a loc that had fell loose over her eye and smoothed it into place gently. He opened the door and stepped out "make sure you lock this" he said as he pulled it closed.

CHAPTER 9

WOO SAT AT the nurses station silently. "You sure you good? You look like shit" Houston said. She was right and Woo felt just as bad as she looked, her locs hung long, wild and free, her face dry and puffy, her eyes red and swole. She glanced at her watch unintentionally giving Houston a view of the bruise on her wrist. "Did Idris do that? I never would've thought" Houston covered her mouth. Woo didn't have the energy to lie but still somewhat defended him "like Toni Morrison said, violent people love violently" she said sadly. A wave of nausea came over her as she made it to the trash can just in time to throw the little she ate for dinner back up. "Damn girl I was just about to say her ass look pregnant, soon as i saw you I could tell, I be knowing" Houston went on. "Is it psychos or dead boos?" she asked concerned. Woo went to the back of the clinic and got a pregnancy test, she disappeared into the bathroom with it. She came back out solemnly answering Houstons question "it can only be Idris and I absolutely can not have his baby".

"Well on another note guess who got escorted out after getting caught fucking an inmate through the cell? "Houston leaned over and did a quick twerk to demonstrate. "Barr ass girl they caught her in the act, all that shit she talked" she shook her head. "I'm not surprised" Woo mustered up not really wanting to talk. "Don't worry girl, I know a place I'll take you" Houston said as she rubbed her back.

Carter was relieving Idris after picking up a day shift. His sons birthday was next week and his baby mom was MIA as always, she was a pill head now and he hadn't heard from her in months. He stood waiting for Idris to come do head count with him and give him the keys. *I know this nigga see me.* West walked up and started a conversation with Carter as he watched Idris out the side of his eye. *Fuck they talking about?* Idris was in a deep conversation with Pitts a rowdy white inmate who was in on two rapes and attempted murder charge. *Did he just point at me?* Carter held his hand up for West to stop talking. "Yo deputy! Lets go!" his voice boomed. Idris nodded at Pitts and arrogantly took his time walking over to Carter and West. "I ain't got time to do head count" he held the keys out. Usually Carter wouldn't care but Idris was on some other shit lately. He ignored the keys "then I ain't taking them shits" he challenged. West uncomfortable with the tension between them spoke up "I'll count with you" he told Carter. Neither man budged "come on man cas I still gotta get to my own floor" he nudged Carter. Idris smirked as he dropped the keys in West hands and walked off. When Carter and West got to Pitts cell he stood defiantly in only his boxers only. "Man you know you gotta be dressed for head count" Carter said. "Fuck you nigger" Pitts hissed. "Yeah, alright get dressed" Carter reiterated. "I'll kill you nigger" Pitts hawked and spit some landing on Carters cheek "Pop the cell" Carter told West icily. West had worked with Carter for years and had never seen him like this. "He ain't worth it man" West pleaded. "Pop the mother fuckin cell" Carter seethed. West stuck the key in the cell and backed away nervously. Carter turned the key and stepped in the cell slamming Pitts without a warning. Inmates rooted as West called for help over the radio. By the time help arrived they had to pull Carter off Pitts who was swollen and bloody.

Woo was down in booking doing a sallyport. It was Wade but he was not himself he was completely incoherent and could barely hold himself up. "Can he walk?" she asked Clark, now a rookie cop who had propped him against the wall like he was furniture. The white cop, his partner spoke instead "yeah, he was running from us and everything" he said dismissively. "Wade you okay? You don't look yourself" she assessed him. Something wasn't right, all of a sudden Wade began convulsing. The deputy in booking caught him to assist his fall and Woo grabbed his head so it didn't hit the floor. She ran into the office and came out with the narcan spraying the midst up Wades nose. He opened his eyes but was completely out of it. Wades health status was a mystery to her other than him being old as hell because he'd refused all medical exams or treatment. "Take him to to the hospital this is not his norm. Hurry" she looked frantically at Clark and his partner neither of them moving fast enough. The next sally port was a rape victim with a shattered jaw, the police she'd reported her rape to discovered she had a warrant and arrested *her!* Woo didn't leave until she saw that the woman talked to the social worker, the woman was suicidal but Woo didn't have the heart to take her clothes and put her in a turtle suit hours after being raped so she watched her in booking until she was assessed by mental health.

Woo was walking to her car. She had been waiting behind so Idris would be gone by the time she left out. She had no idea what had happened with Carter since she had been over in booking. Carter saw her walking and called out to her, he had been sent home for the incident while the higher ups determined his fate. He caught her up on what she had missed leaving her shocked. Ultimately Pitts would be okay just banged up. "That's fucked up, you think Idris gonna get in trouble for putting him up to it?" she asked. "Hell no. He in cahoots with the sheriffs and who knows who else. But he gone get his" Carter said, the last part more to himself than her. He walked her to her car and promised to keep her posted. He watched her pull off and had to shake his head, the one female he had never even slept with and her crazy man was after him. He laughed at the irony as he got in his car and sped off music blasting.

CHAPTER 10

THAT NIGHT NO sooner had she sat her bag down someone was calling a code. It was coming from on of the iso cells. Luckily they hadn't done shift change so they had a full medical staff present. The young female deputy who had called the code had been screaming so they knew it was serious. They found Bandi hanging from a ripped sheet, his light brown skin looked blue and his pants bunched at his ankles. He'd been dead for a while. They cut him down and performed CPR even though they all knew the outcome, such was protocol. The sound of his ribs cracking under the weight of her pumps was a sound she'd never forget, sweat was in her eyes and her back and knees felt like they were on fire. Waste was beginning to pool underneath him and his tongue lagged around hanging from his mouth. She'd just about ran out of breath as the paramedics came and took over but Bandi never regained consciousness. He had been a handful but he was only 31 and well liked by the medical staff. Death was common in the nursing field but losing the young was was not, this time was different mainly because it was unexpected. Bandi was in good health and appeared to be in good spirits despite circumstance. Losing the elderly was not nearly as traumatic. Usually it was followed by a time of suffering to where death was welcome and much more tolerable than the suffering. It was rarely a surprise, first came the smell then the sounds, seasoned nurses could even pinpoint the day. Woo recalled the time she thought she scared her patient to death, literally. Mr. Greene was 80 years old by the time he ended up on the hospice unit he had went from friendly to mean as a snake, to nothing. It felt wrong prolonging the inevitable. He was in constant pain when he wasn't he knocked out on morphine. The pancreatic cancer has dissolved about 100lbs of him but he was still a large man. Woo missed their conversations, instead now she went in cleaned and medicated him, humming along to the music that played on his bedside nightstand. She knew he recognized her due to the fact he still gave her hand a gentle squeeze she'd stand there as long as she had time sometimes pulling up a chair, the whole time his eyes never opened. His last night alive the death rattles could be heard from the hallway. He was soiled but Woo had to wait for her aide to assist her to clean him due to him being in so much pain he winced at the slightest touch. He was laying on four absorbent pads since his entire body was just draining fluid it was even coming out of his skin when Woo placed her hand on his arm an indent was left. They carefully rolled him over and cleaned his backside, rolling up the soiled bedding replacing them with fresh linen a technique the aide was much more efficient at than Woo. Once complete they rolled him back in place he let out a huge sigh, fluids gushed from under him undoing all the cleaning they had carefully done. "He's dead!" The aide shrieked. "Mr. Greene!" Woo bent and said loudly said in his face. "Agh!" His head lifted, eyes and mouth wide open. There he froze eyes and mouth stuck in place. The two girls stood in shock for a moment before acting. Woo attempted to lay him back but the man was solid, cold, hard and unmoving. She checked for a pulse but there was none. She discreetly cracked his window so his soul could find freedom and called the time of death 3:33. The older nurse assured her she'd done of two things scared him to death or he'd passed away when he let that loud sigh and she called him back for a moment. Either way she felt no better about it. His body was still in the same position when the funeral home came. She busied herself straightening up the room so she wouldn't see but the cracks she heard when he was being "adjusted" flat on the stretcher were gruesome.

Medical was grim as they charted the incident and covered all their bases with sadness in their spirits. *Bandi wouldn't kill himself.* A chill went through Woo and she shuddered.

The next night the jail was swarming with higher ups. "The jail investigating the jail, don't make no sense" Mack fussed. Woo was lost in her thoughts. "Hey, I'll be right back. I'm going to go stretch my legs. You want me to do your rounds on the iso floor?" she asked Mack. "Yes Lord. See God is good" Mack started but Woo was already gone.

On the iso floor Woo stopped by to see one of her favorite trustees Poole. He had snapped one day after court and got thrown in iso. He'd been losing weight, braided his beard in tiny plaits and had a spaced out look in his eyes. He'd written 3 page front and back letters to the social worker 4 weeks later he was still in iso. After her, Houston and a few others expressed concern of him deteriorating he was moved to the crazy block. It was too late he beat up 3 people and was thrown right back in iso. He didn't look up at Woo as she spoke to him through the door. She put her hand to the small window before walking away sadly. Poole placed his hand in the spot were hers had been.

"Nobody else bothered to ask me a damn thing and I'm right in the next cell" Cleveland said. Woo was crouched down by the slot on his door. "So you say Idris was in there?"

she clarified. She didn't bother whispering apparently the cameras on this hall had conveniently stopped working a few days ago. "Yup him and the junkie bitch Flores" he told her. "Really?" Woos eyebrows shot up. "Hell yeah that bitch dirty, and she on that shit bad too" he said. "Anybody else know?" she asked. "Just me and you so do right by my cuz" his voice cracking. Woo thought for a second "where is Bandis stash?"

She dropped her pen and watched as it rolled into Bandis empty cell, she waited a few seconds before following it in. All they'd done was put a sign on the door saying *Do Not Use This Cell.* She used her pen to pry into a crack in the tile behind the toilet. Inside was a needle and four vials. She slipped the capped needle along with the vials in her pocket placing the tile back like she'd found it. She went back to Clevelands cell dropping two vials in his hand and discreetly slid the Malcolm X copy through the tray slot. "Guess you ain't no square" he told her. "'People change, this place changes you" she said. "Nah it don't change, just reveal" he told her. "Well I'm whatever it is I need to be when I need to be it" she smiled. "One more thing. Where does Flores cop?" she asked.

"Somebody want you in the conference room, a female called and didn't leave no name" Mack told her once she got back in medical. Woo went to the back of the clinic to stash what she'd taken from Bandis cell. Once in the conference room she was infuriated on see the huge table was empty except for Flores who sat clutching a file. "Where's Keene?" she demanded. She didn't have to answer to Flores. "I was told you're beginning to be a problem" Flores started. Woo stayed next to the door. "You never disclosed your mental disabilities that may get in the way of your job". Woo didn't flinch. "You also know drug use is prohibited" Flores said. *I can't believe Idris told her* she fought to hide her irritation. "Say, whatever happened to your rapist? That case went cold huh. Like father like daughter I suppose" Flores smirked at Woo. She huffed out slamming the door behind her. She ran to the first trash can she saw and began heaving into it. Idris walked up mouth hanging open. "Why didn't you tell me?" he asked sizing her up. She had picked up some weight around her mid section. He reached out for her but she turned and rushed away. Flores exited the conference room. "What the fuck did you say to her? I told you stay out of it, she don't know anything!" he roared pushing her out the way before she could respond.

CHAPTER 11

WOO WAS USING a few of her vacation days to get her mind right. She had considered quitting but then what? To make matters worse she had ran into Clark at a gas station and asked about Wade since he'd never returned *Oh you won't see him no more he never even made it to the hospital* he had told her. *He died? I checked the paper everyday looking for his name and nothing* she said in disbelief. *Oh you won't read about it any where* he has told her emotionless it was all too much. The black bag on the dresser caught her eye. She went over to open it, ready to see what Khalil wanted her to have. A copy of *Art of War*. "Thank you" she whispered through her tears. *You know what to do* a now familiar voice responded.

"Yo that's crazy" Carter said in said in disbelief as he sipped his drink. They'd met up at a bar and she was catching him up on everything minus the baby. She wasn't gonna keep it so no need not with her genes and Idris crazy ass, which was why she was buzzed. She'd misses her confidant and somehow he'd managed to make even this funny. "I wouldn't put it past hem to have dumped Wade somewhere, nothing new" he agreed pouring out a little of his drink for Wade. They chilled a little longer but she couldn't help feeling like she was putting Carter in danger just by them meeting up. She told him she was gonna head out. "Be careful" she gave him a friendly hug and got into her car. "Oh no doubt" he smiled.

Idris walked into his apartment. He'd been parked outside of Woos all evening but she still hadn't returned home. It was driving him crazy not knowing where she was. He wanted to talk to her about the baby. He was ready for a fresh start, he knew he was in over his head moving drugs with Bandi. He didn't regret getting rid of him though, Bandi would've snitched to save himself. But he was ready to settle down at least he knew now she couldn't ignore him for long in her condition. Besides he had way more than enough money to take as much time off as he needed. He sat at the foot of his bed with his head in his hands. He lifted his head when he heard somebody creep up from behind. He turned just in time to see Carter behind him and press the gun to his head. "Bitch ass" Carter mumbled sending one shot through his temple. Carter wiped the gun clean and placed it in Idris hand wrapping his fingers around it. He grabbed the huge duffle bag containing Idris stash he'd removed before Idris got home and placed the silver key on the counter as he walked out.

CHAPTER 12

WOO SAT IN her car reciting a quote from *The art of War. Know yourself and you will win all your battles.* She questioned who she was *a crazy mother and a murderer for a father, that's who I am.* She never thought she'd be in this position again, the first time she'd killed was when she stabbed her rapist to death. His case closed shortly after. Flores was reaching earlier she'd mistakingly said he'd been shot half true, either way Idris betrayed her she thought. What terrified her was the fact she felt no remorse or maybe the rush she felt when she did it. She had no choice she'd subjected herself to burns with how hot her shower after the rape but could not free herself of him. He had forcibly etched himself inside her flesh, inside her spirit she carried around the extra weight of him suffocating her in the weeks following. He had to go. *To know your enemy you must become your enemy* she closed the book. Flores pulled up just as Cleveland said she would. She was in and out in less than 5 minutes. The young boy nodded at Woo from the porch before disappearing back in the rundown house.

Flores was found dead the next morning by her teenage daughter with the needle still in her arm. She injected herself with a lethal hot shot and was dead before she could pull the needle back out. Bandi, Flores, and Idris deaths were all ruled as suicides. Khalils murder was solved when his wallet and gun were recovered at Idris apartment. Hopefully that would bring his family some peace. Wade was never seen again sadly.

A little over a year later Woo stood over a small grave as a lone tear rolled down her cheek. "Keep still lil man and pay your respects" Carter said to his son who was getting restless. "I'ma just take them to the car" he said realizing his son staying still was not gonna happen. "Come to daddy and let your momma say bye to that loud ass bird" Carter said gently lifting the adorable baby boy from Woos arms. The way the sunlight cast off his face made the silver streak that started at his hairline and ended at his lashes sparkle. "I'll miss you Ruby" she said tearfully. Ruby hadn't survived the move to Ghana and passed peacefully in her travel crate. She paused and took in the beauty of the place. There was nothing for her back in Richmond, she was glad she was pushed in a corner and forced out. A soft breeze blew past and danced around her. *Welcome home* her grandmothers voice peaceful in her ear. "I made it" she whispered wiping the tears as they fell.

Willow smiled as she went to catch up with Carter and the boys who'd stopped to wait for her, she loved her new family, she felt whole. She slid her hand into his free hand. "You sure you wanna start over with a ain't shit nigga" he joked. "That depends, you ever consider maybe I ain't shit either" she winked at him.

N. Nichelle is a self taught writer. She is a lifelong bibliophile, wife, mothership to three and nurse by career. She began her first novel *Please don't let me be misunderstood* at 32. As the great Toni Morrison stated "if there's book that you want to read, but hasn't been written yet, you must write it". Currently she resides peacefully in Arizona with her family and many pets.

www.ingramcontent.com/pod-product-compliance
Lightning Source LLC
Chambersburg PA
CBHW071946190726
48293CB00004B/1384